ELMER'S WALK

David McKee

Andersen Press

Elmer the patchwork elephant was sniffing some flowers when some other elephants hurried by. "Come and smell these flowers," Elmer called. "We don't have time, Elmer," said an elephant. "We're hurrying somewhere."

Not long after that, Elmer was looking
at an old tree trunk.
Three crocodiles charged past.
"Hey, crocodiles," called Elmer. "Look, there's
a log pretending to be one of you chaps."
"Another time, Elmer," shouted a crocodile, and
one after another they plunged into the water
and disappeared.

Lion came running past while Elmer was listening to the waterfall.

"Hey ho, Lion," said Elmer. "Come and—"

"I don't have time now, Elmer," Lion interrupted. "I'm late for a very important nap."

Then he was gone.

The monkeys came swinging
through the trees just as Elmer noticed a
spider's web that had captured some drops of rain.
"Look," called Elmer.
"Yes, yes! Lovely! Delightful! Amazing!" said the
monkeys without looking or slowing down.

Continuing his walk, Elmer paused to watch the river play with his reflection. The group of elephants raced by again. "Stop a moment," said Elmer.

Before he could say more, an elephant said, "No time, Elmer. Sorry, we're still hurrying somewhere."

Elmer was alone again.

When the birds flew by, Elmer had no chance to say anything about the rocks he was looking at.

They flew past quickly
with just a, "Hello, Elmer. No time to stop!"
Elmer sighed and walked on.

Suddenly, a noise made Elmer think the elephants were back. It was the hippos.

"Look at the clouds," said Elmer. "There's one that looks like an elephant."

"That's funny, Elmer, so do you," said a hippo. The others laughed and ran on without even a glance at the clouds.

Elmer was watching the
butterflies dance when Tiger galloped by.
"Steady, Tiger," said Elmer.
Tiger slowed and said, "Elephants may not
know about teatime, but tigers certainly do
and I don't intend to miss it. No time to stop.
Sorry, bye."

Later, Elmer met Snake.
"You know, Snake," he said, "it's sad.
Nobody has time to just stop and stare."
"I agree," said Snake. "Sad, very sad."
"For instance," said Elmer. "Look at those flowers.
They have more colours than you and I put
together." But snake had already left.

The elephants rushed by again when Elmer was listening to his echo. He didn't try to stop them. "I know," he said. "You're busy hurrying somewhere." "You are silly, Elmer," an elephant laughed. "Can't you see? We're hurrying back from somewhere." Elmer just sighed.

"Hurry, hurry; hurry, hurry," murmured Elmer
as he strolled on. Then he saw his cousin Wilbur.

"Hello, Wilbur," he said. "What are you doing?"
"Watching the night arrive," said Wilbur.

The cousins stood happily together and
watched the sky darken and fill with stars.

"Shall we count them?" asked Wilbur.
"No," said Elmer. "We haven't the time."